Hazel Townson

HOT STUFF

Illustrated by David McKee

Andersen Press · London

Text © 1991 by Hazel Townson
Illustrations © 1991 by David McKee

First published in 1991
by Andersen Press Limited,
20 Vauxhall Bridge Road, London SW1V 2SA.
This edition published 2002.

British Library Cataloguing in Publication Data available
ISBN 0 86264 931 5

Contents

For Claire Sturges and the staff and pupils of Sinfin Community School, Derby

1

Hotheads, Beware!

A middle-aged, red-headed man and two schoolboys stood on a motorway bridge gazing down at the traffic.

'Just look at that!' Arthur Venger ordered the boys disgustedly. 'Most of those drivers are doing ninety miles an hour, or I'm a dustman. And nose-to-tail, at that.'

'Speed is the curse of civilisation,' declared young Herbie Coswell the genius.

'You've said it!' his friend Kip Slater cried in horror as a van swerved dangerously on to the hard shoulder, avoiding disaster by centimetres.

'Hotheads, that's what they are! The world's full of 'em! Speed maniacs, terrorists, football hooligans . . . all hotheads! Time we did something about it.'

This may have seemed a strangely boastful remark, but Arthur Venger was no ordinary person. An inventor with exceptional talents, he regarded himself as a crusader, trying to right the ills of the world. (A. Venger the Avenger, in fact.) Already he had conducted many campaigns, including one to banish litter and another to make everyone tell the truth by substituting Truthpaste for tooth-paste. Now he was obviously on the verge of a new break-through.

'What could we do about it – cool the hotheads down?' grinned Kip sarcastically, picturing the three of them training cold-water hoses on to the traffic below.

But if he had thought to ridicule Arthur Venger, he had failed. For the red-head's eyes took on a fanatical gleam as he cried, 'Exactly! I've already produced a potion I've christened Koolit, which has instant calming

effects on the brain in such hothead circumstances. Restores to normal with no nasty side-effects. One application lasts for a week or more, but the trouble is, the Koolit has to be massaged into the skin, preferably the scalp, and I don't quite see how I can persuade our hotheads to use it.'

'Why not put it into a shampoo?' suggested Herbie the genius at once. 'Even terrorists have to wash their hair. If you gave the

shampoo some smart packaging, a really cheap price and a stunning perfume, it would take off like a space probe.'

'A shampoo? You know, that's not a bad idea!' Arthur's brain was already whirling with new possibilities.

'And of course,' Herbie went on, 'once word got round how unique this stuff was, people would soon be clamouring for it. Then your price could go up and up.'

Kip Slater gazed at his friend in unstinting admiration.

'Herbie, you're a genius!' he declared.

But of course, Herbie Coswell knew that already.

'Well, there it is!' cried Arthur Venger, holding aloft a bottle containing a pale pink liquid. 'Koolit Shampoo – the product that will change the world.'

He and the boys had been working busily on the preparation in Arthur's bungalow, brewing, measuring and bottling this latest concoction. All that remained was

11

the labelling.

'H'm!' muttered Herbie thoughtfully. 'I'm not keen on the name. I wouldn't choose a

shampoo with a name like Koolit, would you, Kip?'

This was a question Kip had not considered. Now he gave it some thought and decided that, as usual, Herbie was right.

'It needs to be something really tempting. A name that makes people feel they will be getting something more than just a shampoo. Hey, what about "Shangri-la Shampoo"? You know, Shangri-la – that storybook place where nobody ever grows old. Or "Utopia" – the perfect world?' (Not for nothing had the Slaters bestowed on their son a literary name like Kipling.)

'Nothing is soapier
Than Utopia!'
chanted Kip, getting carried away.

'No, no; half the customers won't ever have heard of those places. You need a name everyone's familiar with. Something like "Brainwave".'

'Now, that really *is* a brainwave, Herbie!' cried Arthur delightedly. 'Brainwave Shampoo – the Really Clever Choice!' He stroked the bottle lovingly as he daydreamed of the calm and wonderful new world that was to be.

'Brainwave – The Thinking Person's Shampoo! An Absolute Inspiration!' improved Kip, determined to have *some* say in the matter.

But Herbie brought them both back to earth with a businesslike query: 'Have you tried it out yet?'

'Only on myself,' admitted Arthur. 'But you know what an impulsive hothead I can be at times, and it certainly cooled me down, for nearly a fortnight.'

'Ah yes, but you were expecting it to; you wanted the stuff to work. We ought to try it out on somebody else before we start advertising it. Maybe there's a snag we haven't thought of.'

Herbie could not help remembering the terrible snags that had cropped up in connection with Arthur's Litterwort invention, not to mention the Truthpaste, and felt that 'impulsive' was a very apt description of

Arthur. It was a good thing Kip and Herbie were there to put some order into possible chaos.

'Well, all right; let's think of a few local hotheads we can use as guinea pigs.'

'The Fleming gang!' cried Kip at once, naming a group of local teenage boys who were well-known disrupters of practically everything.

There were five boys in the gang, led by Fatso Fleming, a beefy bully of a lad who regarded it as his mission in life to spoil things for other people.

Herbie was doubtful. 'You'll never get that bunch to use a shampoo just because you ask them to. They're more likely to stuff it down your neck and pour the water after it.'

Kip looked offended. Herbie Coswell wasn't the only one with brains, and he, Kip, intended to stick to his idea.

'They'll use it if Mr Venger pays them,' he declared stubbornly. 'That lot will do anything for money.'

And he was very nearly right.

2

Victims Bewitched

At the Grumpton Rovers' home game the following Saturday, the Fleming gang was much in evidence as usual, draped in ten-foot scarves and other gaudy items. But this time Fatso's four henchmen, their well-washed locks springing merrily round their stripy bobble-caps, behaved impeccably. They had even left their rattles and toilet rolls at home. Only Fatso, who had pocketed Arthur Venger's bribe and then sold the shampoo to his next-door neighbour, shouted abuse and threw missiles and picked fights with rivals in his customary manner. It was obvious he

hadn't washed his hair for weeks, and it took the combined efforts of the other four gang members to simmer him down.

'Cool it, Fatso!' cried one, laying on his leader a gentle but firm restraint.

'Yeah, take it easy, man! We just want to enjoy the game.'

'Let's have a bit of peace for once; a nice quiet, restful afternoon.'

'This is a football match, not World War Three.'

'Would you believe it?' Kip cried gleefully as he, Herbie and Arthur looked down on their victims from higher up in the stand. 'That stuff's an absolute wow!'

'A most satisfactory result!' agreed Arthur. 'In fact, more than satisfactory. I didn't bargain on this knock-on effect of some folks restraining others. We're definitely on to a winner!'

'Hang about!' cautioned Herbie. 'That's only one trial. No true scientist would be satisfied with that. We must make at least two trials, and I think we ought to tackle a reckless driver next.'

This, as it turned out, was where disaster set in, though they were not to know it for several days.

Arthur Venger had a next-door neighbour

called George, who was a travelling salesman for a toffee firm. George, who spent most of his working life behind the wheel, had developed a turn of speed which was second to none, and boasted that he could drive from Grumpton to London in fifty minutes. Considering that the express train took two hours to complete the same distance, this was quite a boast. George was obviously the man for the second experiment.

'You can't offer him shampoo,' protested Kip. 'He's as bald as a basin.'

'Well then, we'll need a second product with the same ingredients. Something a bald man would use. Bath-oil, maybe; or sunscreen lotion, or aftershave.'

'Hair-restorer!' cried Herbie the genius promptly.

'By Jove, you've done it again, Herbie! "Brainwave Hair-restorer"! The very thing! That should tempt old George; he's incredibly vain.'

It certainly did.

George was delighted with Arthur's present, which might save him the cost of the expensive toupée he had been considering buying. He tried out the hair-restorer at once, but was disconcerted to find that not only did he remain as bald as ever, but that day's journey to London took him nearly three hours.

No contra-flows either; unheard of!

As a result of this delay, George lost an order for five thousand packets of Munchibits and was bawled at for half an hour by the Area Manager. Another disaster like that, and he could well lose his job.

'I just couldn't seem to drive any faster,' he told Arthur, 'though there was nothing wrong with the car. It was uncanny.'

Of course, when Arthur heard George's tale of woe he was even more delighted than he had been at the football match. It took a great effort for him to look suitably sympathetic.

'Never mind, George; it could have been worse. You could have lost an order for *ten* thousand packets.'

As soon as the disgruntled George had departed, Arthur rubbed his hands with glee.

'Right!' he told the boys. 'We've had two amazingly successful trials, so now is the moment of truth. I shall contact our local police. When they discover the brilliance of my product they'll snap it up. Think what "Brainwave" will save them in manpower, injuries, vandalism and stress. They'll probably award me a Police Medal, Class One.'

'Or make you Chief Constable,' suggested Kip. 'Shall we come with you?'

'No; police stations are no places for young lads. You two wait for me at the bungalow.'

'Well, hurry up, Mr Venger. We'll have a celebration when you get back.'

Alas! All that glory was just an empty dream.

Chief Inspector Snagg, whom Arthur insisted on seeing – ('Always go right to the top, boys!') – had the best memory in the business, and recalled with vivid clarity the troubles resulting from Arthur's previous attempts to improve the world.

'Not interested!' he told Arthur brusquely. 'Kindly close the door as you leave.'

'We might have known,' moaned Herbie gloomily. 'Genius is never recognised by ordinary mortals until it's nearly too late.

You ask Darwin and Newton and Columbus.'

'We can't; they're dead,' Kip pointed out. 'And it's no use sitting here feeling sorry for ourselves. Let's go down to the snack bar and cheer ourselves up.'

Arthur groaned. Did boys think food was the solution to everything? He declared that nothing in the world would ever cheer him up again, especially not food, but the boys ignored him. They knew very well that Arthur was up on Cloud Nine one minute and down in the depths of gloom the next, and that two cups of tea and a Cornish pasty might make all the difference. As it happened, there was not even any need for refreshments, for the three of them had not been more than a minute in the snack bar when they made an astounding discovery.

3

Villains Befriended

Barney Bloggs and his partner-in-crime, Sam Tuffle, leaned their heads together over the snack bar table like the conspirators they undoubtedly were. They had chosen a secluded corner for the hatching of their latest dastardly scheme, the theft of the newly-discovered Turner painting 'Storm over Skye'. This painting had been unearthed only six months ago in the attic at Grumpton Hall. Some tasteless idiot had rolled up the canvas and dumped it in a filthy umbrella stand, where it had mouldered away for years. In the nick of time, it had been rescued and

lovingly restored, and was at present on display in Grumpton Art Gallery, insured for no less than three million pounds.

Barney and Sam already had a secret buyer for the painting, an American billionaire by the name of Cyrus J. Beefenburger, who collected famous works of art as black velvet collects the fluff. But the really important part of their plan was that the money Cyrus paid would be used to buy bomb-making equipment for their latest terrorist escapade. For Barney and Sam belonged to the 'Freedom for the Potteries' Movement, bent on securing self-rule for this area of Britain. Known as the Hot Pots, they would stop at nothing to achieve their objective, and had already blown up a porcelain effigy of Josiah Wedgwood, two litter-bins, and the wardrobe in which their equipment had been stored.

Now the conspirators were poring over a map which showed the layout of Grumpton Art Gallery. They had rented an empty office next door, and were almost through digging a tunnel which would come up – they hoped –

in the right bit of the Art Gallery building.

As these two villains mumbled over their plans, Kip, who had very sharp ears and was sitting just behind Barney, caught a few vital phrases and began to put two and two together. With frantic hand-signals he tried to convey to Arthur and Herbie the significance of what was happening. Then all three began straining their ears to listen, and Arthur even jotted down notes on the edge of his paper napkin.

Terrorists!

The very worst types of hothead!

Here was a wonderful chance to put the 'Brainwave' plan into action and show the police what was what!

'Hot Pots, of all people!' whispered Herbie disgustedly. 'They're always up to something nasty, but I never thought they'd come to Grumpton.'

'I'm glad they did.' Turning on his most charming smile, Arthur leaned across to the Hot Pots' table and held out a couple of shampoo samples which the police had so snootily ignored.

'Like to try some? It's free. All part of the advance publicity campaign. And it's more than just a shampoo. Clears the head marvellously. Great for creative thinking and forward planning.'

The two conspirators frowned suspiciously.

'Why pick on us?'

'He's not picking on you,' Herbie cut in promptly. 'We're going to give this stuff out to everyone in the snack bar, aren't we, Mr Venger?'

'And in the street outside,' added Kip.

Arthur showed some astonishment. He had not intended free gifts on that sort of scale. However, he could see that the Hot Pots were distrustful, so he had to agree. After all, once he had proved his point to the police he would be able to name his own price. Resignedly, he handed his car keys over to the boys, who fetched a whole crate of 'Brainwave' and began to distribute it among the customers. The ladies seemed particularly pleased, and snatched up the samples eagerly.

Barney and Sam relaxed a little, though they still kept Arthur under careful scrutiny. Was he a member of MI5 in disguise? In the end, judging from his looks, his messily crumbled Cornish pasty and his two school-boy companions, they decided not, and began to take the product seriously. Barney felt Sam could do with his head clearing, and Sam felt Barney could use some help with the forward planning, so each accepted Arthur's gift on the other's behalf. Upon which, our three heroes speedily left the snack bar. Arthur rushed excitedly back to the police station with his news of the conspiracy, and the boys went home for tea, promising to meet Arthur again afterwards.

Chief Inspector Snagg glared at Arthur Venger and was not amused. Already that week he had seen enough cranks and crack-pots to last him until Judgement Day, and here was one daring to come back a second time. Arthur managed to gasp out only a few hasty phrases before he was despatched with even more speed and sarcasm than before.

When the boys returned to Arthur's bunga-low after tea, they were very disappointed.

'So you see,' Arthur told them angrily, 'it's up to us! We'll have to catch those villains ourselves and show the Force a thing or two. Snagg will be begging for our co-operation before we've done.'

'Great!' cried Kip. 'A taste of real adven-ture at last!'

But Herbie the genius was not so sure. 'It's a no-win situation. If the "Brainwave" works there won't be a crime after all, and we won't be able to prove a thing. If it doesn't work, we've lost anyway.'

Arthur looked stricken, but Kip refused to be daunted.

'Well, let's assume they won't wash their hair just yet. They'll steal the picture first. If we catch them at it, the police will have to start taking notice.'

'All right,' agreed Herbie, 'at least we can warn the Curator that the Turner is about to be stolen. Then maybe we can help him catch the villains red-handed.'

'Why is it,' wondered Arthur Venger gloomily, 'that every time I have a brilliant idea there's a flaw in it somewhere? I don't know why I bother.'

'Courage, Mr Venger!' Herbie waved a clenched fist in the air. 'If this stuff works, then even if we have no proof, we'll know we cooled the hotheads down and probably saved a lot of lives. We'll be unsung heroes – benefactors of mankind.'

'Cor!' said Kip.

4

Curator Bedevilled

By the time Arthur had left the police station for the second time, the Art Gallery was closed. So at Herbie's suggestion they tracked down the Curator at his home, two streets away.

'Put your minds at rest,' the Curator announced from his doorstep with a self-satisfied smile. 'That Turner is very well protected. We have no less than three different alarms concealed around it, besides an experienced Night Patrol. Theft is an absolute impossibility.'

As he spoke, there came the sound of a

nearby explosion, followed by a mighty clang-
ing noise, then a high-pitched buzz and
finally a mechanical wailing sound which was
cruel on the ears. Shouts and running feet

could be heard in all directions. The shocked Curator, already suspecting the worst, fled in the direction of the tumult, and the boys and Arthur followed him.

In a small room at the back of the Art Gallery, where the Turner had been hung in solitary splendour, two uniformed members of the Night Patrol were slumped in a daze on the floor; a large chunk of wall had been blown out, leaving bare wires sprouting dustily; rubble lay scattered everywhere, and the Turner itself was gone.

'Too late; too late!' wailed Arthur. 'Those Hot Pots must have come straight here from the snack bar whilst I was wasting time hanging around at the police station.'

'Never mind,' Herbie consoled. 'Those Hot Pots will have to wait for the hue and cry to die down before they can get rid of the painting. They'll have to hide themselves away for a few days. A perfect opportunity for them to wash their hair. It must be full of plaster dust.'

At this point, further commotion heralded

36

6

the arrival of the police. Four officers rushed into the gallery, headed by Chief Inspector Snagg. Taking in the situation at a glance, the grim-faced Chief Inspector gestured dramati-

37

cally at Arthur Venger.

'Grab that man!' he cried. 'I need him to help us with our enquiries,' whereupon a couple of constables bore down on Arthur.

'Hey!' cried Herbie, outraged. 'You can't do that! Mr Venger isn't the thief. He went to warn the Curator that the painting might be stolen.'

'That's true; he did,' agreed the Curator grudgingly, although he could not help feeling that Arthur Venger was mixed up in the outrage somewhere.

'And how did he know?' sneered the Chief Inspector. 'Second sight, I suppose? Don't tell me you weren't suspicious? Why, the fellow is already notorious as a troublemaker, and he's just been shouting threats all over my police station about that painting being stolen. He certainly knows *something* about it.'

'A pity you didn't arrest him earlier, then,' observed the Curator drily, 'if you were so sure he was up to no good.'

'Let's be reasonable!' pleaded Herbie. 'What thief would warn the police in advance? It's the last thing he'd do.'

'Not if he was a crackpot, like this one.'

'It's not the crackpots you should be looking for; it's Hot Pots,' cried Kip. 'They stole that painting to finance their next bombing campaign.'

'Hot Pots? Don't make me laugh! Hot Pots wouldn't waste their time in a place like Grumpton. Anyway, who asked for *your* opinion? Look, you two kids had better clear off before I decide to hold on to you as well,' growled Snagg, who had not so far connected the two boys directly with Arthur Venger. 'Go on, hop it!'

'We might have been able to help you, but we know when we're not wanted. Come on, Kip!'

'Are we just going to leave Mr Venger to his fate?' worried Kip as they fled along the corridor.

''Course not! We're going to carry on the good work and track down those villains ourselves, before they plant any bombs. Then the police will have to release Mr Venger. If we stay here arguing until we get arrested we won't be able to help him at all.'

He hurried Kip out into the street.

'Yeah, that all sounds very noble, but where do we start?'

'With this!' Glancing furtively about him to make sure no one was watching, Herbie held out his hand, in the palm of which lay a crumpled white business-card.

'I just found it on the floor, near where the painting used to hang.'

Kip stared in surprise at the card, which read:

SAM TUFFLE – PLUMBER
2, Slag Buildings, Hanslem,
Nr. Stoke-on-Trent. Tel: Hanslem 4690.

5

Conspirators Becalmed

Barney and Sam leaned over the table in their basement flat and stared in bewildered pride at the Turner canvas they had just unrolled.

'You mean to say this thing's worth three million pounds? No kidding?'

'More! Three million's what it's insured for. But I'll bet if you put it up for auction you'd get bids of twice as much.'

'We're in the wrong business, Barney.'

'Go on, then,' Barney grinned, 'if you think you can paint pictures worth that much I'm not stopping you. It would save us a lot of digging and blasting.'

'Well, we can't put it up for auction. You're sure old Beefenburger will give us our price? We need every penny to buy that bomb-making stuff.'

'No problem. He can't wait to hang that Turner in his secret gallery. But we can't hand it over until next Friday. We'll have to lie low and let the hue and cry die down first.'

Sam Tuffle's face fell. 'This is the bit I hate, hanging around with nothing to do, and all

tensed up in case something goes wrong.'

'We'll survive; we always do. First we'll hide the picture, then we'll get the draughts board out. So stop moaning.'

'Draughts, at a time like this? We'd do better to work on a bit of forward planning first. Which reminds me, your hair's full of plaster dust. Time you gave it a good shampoo.'

'You've some room to talk!' sneered Barney. 'Seen yourself in the mirror lately? How you expect to keep a clear head with all that muck in your hair . . . '

Meantime, Herbie had telephoned the number on the plumber's business card, asking to speak to Sam Tuffle. Sam's wife had answered with the news that her husband was away in Grumpton for a few days on business.

Herbie tried to sound devastated. 'Our headmaster needs a lot of work doing at school,' he said (which was perfectly true, though it was work of an academic, rather than a plumbing, nature). 'Do you happen to know where your husband is staying? It's very urgent – now or never.'

'Hang about – he wrote it down on a bit of paper. Yes; here it is. "Basement Flat, 3, Wicksteed Court, Grumpton." He's not on the 'phone there, though, and he'll be out till late on a plumbing job.'

'Some job, plumbing the depths of wickedness,' sneered Kip as the two boys started out towards Wicksteed Court.

'Hey! Those two kids have turned up again!' cried Barney, peering through the basement fanlight as he rubbed his hair dry with one of Sam's tee-shirts.

'What kids?'

'The two with that geezer who gave us the shampoo. You can see 'em through the railings, loafing about outside.'

'So what? It's a free country. Maybe they're still giving their samples out on the streets. It's great stuff, that shampoo; made me feel really good, it has.'

Sam stretched lazily in front of the gas fire.

His hair was dry already, being thinner on top than Barney's.

'I didn't altogether like the look of that little red-head. Suppose they're on to us?'

'What, a doddery old bloke and a couple of kids? Be your age, Barney.'

'Well, if those two are not gone in five minutes . . . '

'Relax, will you?' Sam yawned. 'There's nothing to worry about. All we have to do is sit here comfortably until Friday, then go off and collect the money.' Suddenly, Sam sat up. 'Hey, listen – I've just had a brainwave. When we *have* collected the money, why don't we just clear off abroad somewhere, buy a nice little villa in the sun and live happily ever after, instead of rushing about like a couple of crazy hotheads, risking our necks with our own explosives? Who cares about Freedom for the Potteries anyway?'

Barney threw down the sodden tee-shirt.

'Say that again!'

Sam said it again, and slowly, very slowly, Barney began to smile.

6

Kip Belaboured

'What good does it do us, knowing where the villains are?' asked Kip. 'We can't go in and snatch the painting back; they'd murder us. And we can't wait here until they come out. It could be days, and my mum will slay me if I'm late home.'

'Our best hope,' pondered Herbie, 'is to create an emergency that will make them come out. Suppose they thought the building was on fire? They'd come out then all right, and the first thing they'd rescue would be that valuable painting. They'd rush out clutching it like a baby. They'd be off their guard and

47

we could snatch it from them, easy as picking a daisy.'

Kip looked shocked. 'Surely you're not thinking of . . . ?'

'Burning the place down? No; I don't think we need to go that far,' Herbie grinned. 'Just a little hint, a mere suggestion, will do the trick.'

As he spoke, Herbie was examining the outside of the house. It was a solid stone four-storey building that had seen better days. The woodwork badly needed a coat of paint; the windows were dirty, and the curtains even dirtier. Half a dozen steps led up to the front door, and a row of bell-pushes showed no less than five different tenants' names.

'One of them is bound to be on the 'phone. Let's pick the most unusual name first, so there won't be so many to hunt through in the directory.'

'Jones – Williams – Bradshaw – Emerald – Scott,' Kip read. 'So it has to be Emerald.'

They sought out the nearest telephone

kiosk and found only one Emerald listed. As they had hoped, the address was 3, Wicksteed Court.

Herbie was soon dialling the Emerald number and announcing in a panic-stricken voice that there might be a bomb in the building, and could Mr Emerald kindly make sure the building was cleared at once?

Mr Emerald hammered frantically on the door of the basement flat at 3, Wicksteed Court.

'Anybody home? Can you hear me in there? We're clearing the building; there's a bomb scare.'

Barney glanced up from the draughts board. He was just about to win another game, which meant Sam would owe him five pounds fifty pence.

'Don't panic!' he called back. 'It's sure to be a false alarm.'

After all, if there was any bomb scare in that building it would be down to him and Sam. They were the terrorists, weren't they?

'It's no false alarm. The cops are on their way. This place is going to go up like the price of petrol, and you can't say I didn't warn you.'

Sam jumped up, managing to knock over the draughts board. He had turned several shades paler.

'Hear that, Barney? We'd best be off.'

'Too true!' Even Barney looked scared. If

the police were on their way, this was no place in which to be lying low. A thorough search of the premises would be made. Besides, Barney suddenly found it uncomfortable to be on the receiving end of a bomb scare for once. Bombs could be dangerous!

'Quick! Out the back way,' he ordered, and Sam was only too eager to obey.

They were halfway across the allotments, on their way to the railway station for a train home to Hanslem, when Barney suddenly stopped and gave an agonising wail.

'Hey, Sam—we forgot the picture!'

The boys were keeping a careful watch on 3, Wicksteed Court, Kip at the back and Herbie at the front. So Kip spotted the escaping Hot Pots at once. Whistling the pre-arranged signal, he gave chase across the allotments, hoping Herbie would follow.

For once, it began to look as though Herbie had blundered. Far from being able to snatch the picture, as Herbie had suggested, Kip could see that the villains were empty-handed. However, he did wonder if perhaps one of them had wrapped the Turner canvas round his middle, like a bullet-proof vest, or even stuffed it up his trouser leg. At any rate, picture or no picture, Kip was determined to keep up with the Hot Pots to see where they were heading.

He had just decided that their destination must be the railway station, when he felt a

heavy hand on his shoulder. Thinking this was Herbie who had caught him up at last, he turned eagerly – but fell instantly into the arms of Fatso Fleming who had been trailing him for some time.

'Right, you wimpy little pest!' cried Fatso, man-handling his victim with gusto. 'I'll teach you to set that red-headed pal of yours on to my friends. Knocked all the life out of 'em, he has, him and his stupid shampoo. Must be drugged, that stuff. And it was you put him on to us. So now you're gonna pay for your fun. Consider yourself kidnapped.'

7

Fatso Belittled

Herbie rounded the corner of Wicksteed Court to see his friend struggling in the brawny grasp of Fatso Fleming. Herbie gave a loud shout of anger, at which the two Hot Pots, a long way ahead, looked back over their shoulders.

Then everything happened at once. Herbie threw himself at Fatso's back and tried to wrench him away from Kip. Fatso dealt Herbie a nasty blow with one hand while twisting Kip's arm with the other. And the two Hot Pots, taking in this scene of violence which they had now come to abhor, turned and raced to the rescue without a second's hesitation.

'You great bully! Pick on somebody your own size!'

'You can't treat young kids like that. Who do you think you are?'

Together the Hot Pots seized Fatso Fleming and shook him like a duster.

'Run, while you've got the chance!' Sam shouted to the boys. But Kip and Herbie had no intention of escaping. They were supposed to be catching criminals, not running away. And anyhow, it would be undignified to have to flee from a bully like Fatso.

All the same, it was a bewildering situation. Even Herbie Coswell the genius had to admit that he didn't know what to do next. How could you betray a couple of guys who had just rescued your best friend from a terrible fate?

Whilst he was still wondering what to do, the matter was decided for him. It was Fatso who broke free and ran away, faster than would have seemed possible with his bulk. It

was obvious he would not be back again in a hurry. Whereupon the Hot Pots dusted off their hands and rapidly continued their journey to the station.

Herbie's indecision had proved fatal.

'Hey, wait a minute!'

The boys did give chase but were only just in time to see the Hot Pots leap on to the Hanslem train, where both stood waving happily from a rapidly-disappearing window, like a couple of kids on holiday. For Barney and Sam were villains no longer, but were now off home, all eager to make fresh attempts at a reasonably normal family life.

They had even come to terms with the loss of the picture and their villa in the sun.

'We'd never have got away with it,' admitted Barney, closing the train window at last. 'And even if we had, we'd have felt hunted for the rest of our lives.'

'Anyway, there's our kids' schooling to think of.'

'And black puddings; can't get those abroad.'

'And Blackpool illuminations.'

'And Hanslem United are in with a chance of the Cup this year.'

'Yeah, I've come to the conclusion that crime doesn't pay,' Sam stated smugly, just at the moment when Herbie Coswell was saying to Kip Slater: 'I've come to the conclusion that they must have left that picture in the flat.'

8

Venger Befuddled

Police Constable Ball was busily searching the basement flat at 3, Wicksteed Court. He had already whizzed through all the drawers and cupboards, peered under beds and sink, even upended the chairs and had the back off the television set. Now he stood by the table, regarding it with distaste. On the filthy tablecloth were piles of dirty pots (most of them full of damp cigarette-ash), a well-used draughts board, and a sauce bottle caked with drips. Constable Ball had already looked under the table and found nothing, but now, as a last resort, he lifted the teapot lid.

'Oh, come on, Fred!' cried his companion, Police Constable Cheyne, fresh from searching the next room. 'You won't find a bomb in there.'

As he spoke, there was a tap at the door and Herbie Coswell's head appeared, closely followed by Kip Slater's.

'Excuse us—!'

'Out!' cried Cheyne fiercely. 'You've no business in here. These premises have been evacuated.'

'We're just going,' soothed Herbie, 'but before we do, how would you like to get promoted?' He was already casting inquisitive glances all around the room.

'You know that missing Turner painting? Well, we think it's somewhere in this flat,' explained Kip.

Constable Cheyne saw red.

'I don't know what you kids are up to, but you'd better beat it, quick. I've got a very nasty temper when I'm roused.'

Ignoring the threat, Herbie went on thoughtfully: 'Where would you hide a paint-

61

ing in a room like this? How about - under the tablecloth?'

Cheyne looked ready to explode.

'Look, I won't tell you again. This is an emergency.'

He began advancing upon the boys. But Constable Ball, who had just put the teapot lid down on the table, suddenly started patting the cloth in all directions. Then, seeing visions of his sergeant's stripes at last, he began frantically clearing away the dishes and stacking them in the sink. While Cheyne spluttered indignant protests, Constable Ball whipped off the cloth - to reveal, laid flat beneath it, 'Storm over Skye' in all its priceless glory.

'You see?' cried Kip triumphantly. 'My friend Herbie's a genius. It doesn't do to ignore what he says.'

'Talking of emergencies,' smiled Herbie complacently, 'is that a big enough bombshell for you, then?'

'What now?' asked Kip when the two constables had made an excited departure with the painting. 'Do we take that business-card to Chief Inspector Snagg?'

'In a word – no!'

'But what about Mr Venger? Suppose Snagg still thinks he's mixed up in the theft? How are we supposed to get him off the hook?'

'Snagg wouldn't take any notice if we gave him the card. He'd probably throw it straight

into his waste-paper basket. And anyway, do you realise those two so-called villains saved your skin? The "Brainwave" has obviously had its effect on them, and it would be a mean trick to get them punished for that.'

'Yeah, I suppose so,' agreed Kip reluctantly.

'Let Chief Inspector Snagg find his own clues, I say,' Herbie went on, tearing the business-card into shreds and stuffing it down a drain. 'Even somebody so stubborn will have to find Mr Venger innocent in the end. And just wait till Snagg gets positive proof that the "Brainwave" really does work wonders, turning villains into sober citizens, or even heroes, at the drop of a blob. He'll end up licking Mr Venger's boots. They all will-judges, prison warders, parliament, prime minister, even the villains themselves. Because you know, Kip, it's the greatest invention since the micro-chip.'

But Kip had stopped listening. Observant as ever, he had just spotted across the road a truly chilling sight.

Arthur Venger was glad to be home. His ordeal, 'helping police with their enquiries', had left him tired and frustrated. Although the painting had now been found, and Snagg had had to release him, he felt no less miserable. For nobody would believe in the wonderful properties of Arthur's 'Brainwave' shampoo, and he was almost ready to pour the whole lot down the sink. His experiment was a failure, as usual. He had actually collected together several crates of bottles with destruction in mind, when suddenly there was a knock at the door, and Arthur's neighbour, George, burst in without waiting for an invitation.

'Hey, Arthur, it works!' cried George excitedly. 'It's growing, Arthur! Look at my hair – it's growing again!'

George bent his head to show off the promising new crop of hair across what had been a completely bald patch.

'Even my moustache is three times as grand.'

For a moment, Arthur was puzzled. Then

he remembered that in George's case the 'Brainwave' had been labelled a 'hair-restorer'. But it wasn't really a hair-restorer—was it?

Apparently it was!

'My goodness gracious!' cried Arthur, peering short-sightedly at George's scalp. 'Why, this stuff must be worth a fortune! And to think I almost poured it down the sink!'

'My thatch started growing on the second day,' George explained happily. 'I'd almost given up hope. I've tried so many so-called wonder products, and they've all turned out failures, so I wasn't really expecting marvels. But then Eureka! All of a sudden, there it was – my first tuft of new hair. And after that it spread faster than fireweed. I can still hardly believe it.'

Arthur sat down heavily.

'I know how you feel,' he said. It was hard to take in this latest unexpected success. But slowly it began to dawn on him that he had made it at last. Hair-restorer was something the public *would* accept. (Even Snagg, who was noticeably reluctant to remove his hat.) After many ingenious but blighted experiments, Arthur would be rich and famous; not quite in the way he had hoped, but at least this latest success would enable him to go on working. One day he would really transform the world, but in the meantime this wasn't a bad beginning - a genuine hair-restorer. It would make countless people happy, and restore their confidence as well as their coiffures. Why, he might even use some of the stuff himself, now he was getting thin on top. He felt ten years younger already! Just wait until the boys heard what had happened!

As if on cue, Herbie and Kip crashed through the garden gate at that moment, and came running towards the house in a state of great agitation.

'Mr Venger! Mr Venger! We've got terrible news!'

'Hurry up and flee!'

'Out the back way, quick!'

'There isn't a moment to lose!'

Arthur looked up in amazement. Kip and Herbie didn't usually panic like this. What on earth could be the matter? Then he saw, advancing upon his bungalow behind the boys, an angry army brandishing brooms,

umbrellas, garden forks and an ingenious variety of other weapons. An army of Grumpton ladies – every one of them thickly bearded!

About the Author

Hazel Townson was born in Lancashire and brought up in the lovely Pendle Valley. An Arts graduate and Chartered Librarian, she began her writing career with *Punch* while still a student. Reviewing some children's books for *Punch* inspired her to write one herself. Over fifty of her books have so far been published and she has written scripts for television. *The Secrets of Celia* won a 'best children's book' prize in Italy and *Trouble Doubled* was shortlisted for a prize in the North of England. She also chairs the selection panel of the Lancashire Children's Book of the Year Award. Hazel is a regular visitor to schools, libraries and colleges and her books have been described as 'fast-moving and funny'. She is widowed with one son, one daughter and four grandchildren.

The Speckled Panic
Hazel Townson
Illustrated by David McKee

When Kip Slater buys *truth*paste instead of
*tooth*paste, he and his friend Herbie soon realise
the sensational possibilities of the purchase.
They plan to feed the truthpaste disguised in a
cake to the guest of honour at their school
Speech Day but, unfortunately, the headmaster
eats the cake first . . .

'A genuinely amusing quick-moving story'
British Book News

ISBN 0 86264 828 9
paperback

The Choking Peril
Hazel Townson
Illustrated by David McKee

Kip and Herbie team up again with Arthur
Venger, the inventor, in an attempt to reform
Grumpton's litterbugs. At the Grumpton
Carnival they distribute free gifts concealing
seeds of a fast-growing weed called Litterwort,
calculating that the wrappings will be discarded
by an untidy public. Next morning the town is
completely choked with Litterwort which has a
wonderful perfume. Far from repelling the
Grumptonians and teaching them a lesson,
the Litterwort attracts people from far and
wide . . .

'Crisp and rib-tickling'
Junior Bookshelf

ISBN 0 86264 930 7
paperback

The One-Day Millionaires
Hazel Townson
Illustrated by David McKee

Arthur Venger, inventor of the notorious
'Truthpaste', has a brilliant new scheme to
make everyone feel more generous. But when
villains cash in on his idea to make a fortune
for themselves, chaos ensues.

'A funny and fast-paced story for fluent readers'
Independent on Sunday

ISBN 0 86264 835 1
paperback

Coughdrop Calamity
Hazel Townson
Illustrated by David McKee

Inventor Arthur Venger and his two young
helpers produce a cure for the common cold,
but they have reckoned without the
unscrupulous Bruno Kopman who will go to
any lengths to preserve his Comical Cough Sweet
business – (a joke on every wrapper). Also hot
on the trail is Doctor Yess who wants the cure to
sell to his rich Harley Street patients. Theft,
kidnapping, corny jokes and mayhem lead to a
devastating conclusion.

ISBN 0 86264 834 3
paperback

Disaster Bag
Hazel Townson
Illustrated by David McKee

Colin Laird is seriously worried about the state
of the world. Disasters are happening all
around him, and he decides to acquire a Disaster
Bag filled with all the equipment he might need
in an emergency. Only then does he begin to
feel safe. But how could he possibly guess that
a terrorist would slip a bomb into his bag when
he wasn't looking . . .?

'One of Townson's best'
Books for Keeps

ISBN 0 86264 524 7
paperback

Trouble on the Train
A Lenny and Jake Adventure
Hazel Townson
Illustrated by Philippe Dupasquier

On a train trip to a Manchester museum, Lenny
overhears a sinister-sounding conversation. Has
he stumbled across a plot to blow up the train?
He tries to pass on a warning, but nobody will
believe him. So he and Jake take matters into
their own hands, ending up in a life-
threatening situation from which they have to
be rescued by a *girl!*

This is the fifteenth story in Hazel Townson's
popular *Lenny and Jake* series. The last story,
The Clue of the Missing Cuff-link, was praised by
the *Independent on Sunday* as a 'fast, funny and
hugely entertaining read'.

ISBN 0 86264 624 3
paperback

TROUBLE DOUBLED
including
Dads at the Double and Double Snatch
Hazel Townson

Two exciting mysteries by Hazel Townson are combined in this paperback original.

Dads at the Double
After meeting at a Schools Drama Festival, Paul and Sara, who live at opposite ends of the country, begin a correspondence. But their letters gradually uncover a horrifying truth which could devastate the lives of both families.

Double Snatch
Angela's weekend visits to her estranged detective dad involve her not only in his case-load but also in a frightening drama which puts her best friend's life at risk.

'The action is artfully advanced through correspondence'
Daily Telegraph

ISBN 0 86264 710 X
paperback